THE PERILS OF PIERRE
BOOK 3
By Ian Janssen
Illustrated by susan ruby k

Published by
WEE CREEK PRESS
www.weecreekpress.com
An Imprint of
WHISKEY CREEK PRESS
PO Box 51052
Casper, WY 82605-1052
www.whiskeycreekpress.com
Copyright 2014 by *Ian Janssen*

Ebook ISBN: 978-1-61160-994-3
Print ISBN: 978-1-61160-995-0

Cover Artist and Illustrator: Susan Ruby K
Editor: Jan Janssen
Line Editor: Steve Womack
Interior Design: Jim Brown
Printed in the United States of America

DEDICATION

This book is dedicated to Jan, my wife, best friend and editor.

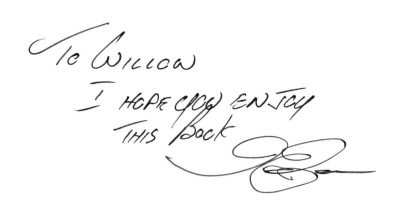

To Willow
I hope you enjoy
this book

THE PERILS
of
PIERRE
Book 3

"BONES OR STONES"

Polly, the crow and Pierre, the fox were sitting on the cliffs over-looking Loon Lake, in the Northern Forest, trying to find something to do. They were enjoying the nice, sunny day, but were getting bored. They needed an adventure to pass the rest of the day.

"Polly, lets go back to where the men are building the road to T Lake," Pierre said. "It's always an adventure when we go down to that end of the lake. Besides, there's a good chance we can find some food there, too!"

"Pierre," Polly said, "remember the last time we were there? You got caught in a cage and had to be rescued! So, I don't think so. We must be able to find something *else* to do."

But while Polly was talking, Pierre had already headed out in a full run for the west end of the lake. Polly followed after Pierre, flying low to the ground around the trees. She wouldn't be able to see Pierre from the air, as the forest was too thick. She just *knew* Pierre was going to get into trouble again!

Pierre had already headed out in a full run

Polly finally caught up to Pierre at Cedar Bay. She called out to him. "Pierre, stop for a minute!" The mischievous red fox came to a halt.

Polly was annoyed. "Pierre, must you take off like that while I'm talking? I was trying to remind you that you got into trouble the last time, and you'll probably get into trouble again! Don't you remember the trap I had to free you from? And the man who soaked me with water, and chased you away from the cook shack?"

"Everything turned out okay the last time. No trap can hold *me*. After all, I'm a cunning fox, and with your help, we find solutions to all the problems I encounter," replied Pierre. "We will this time too, because we know what to expect this time."

Polly couldn't argue with Pierre's logic, so the two friends continued on to the west end of Loon Lake. Finally, they arrived at the clearing that would soon be a road. There were no workers to be seen, so they started to explore the area.

Pierre saw the big yellow skidder but this time it was not billowing black smoke. Then they went to the cook shack, but it was closed and there was no one around. Pierre was looking for a way in when Polly saw a truck coming towards them, so she yelled to Pierre. "Pierre, someone is coming, run!"

Pierre was too busy to pay attention to Polly. He continued to look for a way into the cook shack. There was no way in, it was all locked up.

Pierre ran around the compound, investigating the other trailers and buildings, searching for something to eat. "I know there *has* to be some food here, and I'm sure I can find a way into the cook shack, or one of these other trailers." Pierre continued his quest for an easy meal.

Polly looked at Pierre and said, "You know, your stomach is going to get you in trouble again, Pierre. We have to get out of here now, before the men in that truck get here."

Pierre knew Polly was right. He gave up his search for a way into the trailers, and headed down the road towards T Lake. Soon he came to an area that was freshly dug up by the big machines. He saw something sticking out of the ground that looked like a bone. The biggest bone he had ever seen! He raced over to it and immediately started digging at the bone, trying to find out how big it was. He was digging madly when Polly caught up to him.

Polly was curious about Pierre's behavior. "Pierre, what have you found?"

The biggest bone he had ever seen!

"I found a huge bone and I'm trying to dig it out so I can take it into the forest!" said Pierre. "I've never seen a bone this big before. It must have been a monster!"

Polly looked puzzled and said, "That just looks like an old rock, it's not a bone. Besides, there's no animal in the forest *that* big."

"Sure, it's a bone," said Pierre. "See? This is the largest rib I've ever seen. It's so big, I don't think I can get it out and carry it into the bush without help!"

Polly studied what Pierre had found and still thought it looked like stone. It didn't look like a bone to her. She told Pierre she thought it was stone but he didn't answer her. He was too busy digging at his find.

Soon Pierre stopped and looked at Polly. "I think you're right, it has to be stone. It sure *looks* like a bone, but I've never seen a bone stuck in rock before." Pierre was not happy. He started to walk away from his find, with his tail drooping, and headed towards the flat rock at the west end of the lake.

Polly asked Pierre what was wrong, and why was he so sad.

"Don't worry," said Polly.

"I'm sure you'll find a good meal soon."

"I thought I had found a good meaty bone to eat. I'm upset I was fooled by a stone that looked like a bone."

"Don't worry," said Polly, "I'm sure you'll find a good meal soon."

Just then, the work site started to come to life. Machinery started to run and more trucks were arriving at the compound that Polly and Pierre had just left.

Pierre got excited. "Hey, maybe the cook shack will be open soon and I'll be able to sneak something to eat from there after all. I know enough to avoid that trap, and we know how to distract the man in the cook shack."

Polly rolled her eyes and said, "Here we go again. What kind of trouble are you going to get into this time, Pierre?"

Just then Polly saw two men walking towards them so she warned Pierre. They hid under a large cedar tree that had branches down to the ground, giving them a great hiding spot where they could see and listen to what was taking place. They heard the two men talking, and saw them standing over the spot where Pierre had been digging earlier.

They hid under a large cedar tree

that had branches down to the ground.

The man in the white hat was talking to the man in the green hat, saying, "Do you remember when those two kids from down the lake, Keenan and Ehren, showed us that impression in the flat rock at the end of the lake that looked like a dinosaur footprint? Well, I think we found the dinosaur that made that footprint! This has to be a dinosaur fossil of some kind, so we'll have to work around it, so we don't damage it."

From their hiding spot under the cedar tree, Polly and Pierre watched as the men pointed to Pierre's stone bone. The two forest friends looked at each other in surprise. So, they had *both* been right! Pierre's bone really *was* a bone, but now it was something called a 'fossil', and more like stone!

And somehow, the two boys from the green cabin had known about the dinosaur! Polly said to Pierre, "Isn't it funny how those kids always seem to get involved in all of our adventures?"

"Isn't it funny how those kids always seem to get involved in all of our adventures?"

ABOUT THE AUTHOR

My name is Ian Janssen and I reside in Elliot Lake, Ontario, Canada with my wife, Jan. We have two grown children who have provided us with 4 lovely grandkids who appear in my stories. The location for *The Perils of Pierre* stories is based on our cottage near Thessalon, Ontario, Canada. So far, there are 5 books in the series and more are planned. This is the third book in the series, published by Wee Creek Press.

I was a police officer for 31 years and a home Inspector for almost 6 years. From this, the only writing I did was technical report writing. This series of books is my first venture into writing for entertainment. Pierre and Polly's escapades were originally for the entertainment of my grandkids, but through the encouragement of family, I submitted them for publication.

About The Illustrator

Susan Ruby K is a freelance artist residing in Northern Ontario, Canada. www.yuneekpix.com

For your reading pleasure, we invite you to visit our web bookstore

An Imprint of Whiskey Creek Press

WEE CREEK PRESS

www.weecreekpress.com

CPSIA information can be obtained
at www.ICGtesting.com
Printed in the USA
LVIC01n0810040314
375695LV00002B/3